Amelia Bedelia & FRIENDS

Paint the Town

Daisy

me!

Holly

Joy

Clay

Skip

Rose

Wade

Cliff

Dawn

Heather

Penny
Angel

Amelia Bedelia

& FRIENDS

Paint the Town

me ↗

by Herman Parish

pictures by Lynne Avril

Greenwillow Books

An Imprint of HarperCollins Publishers

Thanks to the real Jackie,
Jacqueline Ehle Inglefield, one fantabulous artist!

Art was created digitally in Adobe Photoshop.

Amelia Bedelia is a registered trademark of Peppermint Partners, LLC.

Library of Congress Control Number: 2020940481

ISBN 978-0-06-296187-7 (hardback)—ISBN 978-0-06-296186-0 (paperback)

21 PC/BRR 10 9 8 7 6 5 4

First Edition

 Greenwillow Books

For Margaret,

who finds art everywhere

—H. P.

For Leslie and Tony,

who allowed me to cover their walls

with paintings and who bring food to my door

when I'm painting Amelia Bedelia! —L. A.

Amelia Bedelia

Finally

Joy

Clay

Heather

Cliff

Wade

Dawn

Skip

Angel

Penny

Contents

Chapter 1

Treasure Hunter?

Amelia Bedelia's stomach was scolding her. Loudly. It rumbled, *When will you feed me?*

She turned to her father and asked, "When will Mom be home?"

"That's the third time you've asked me in the last ten minutes," said her father.

"The only time I can think about is dinnertime," said Amelia Bedelia. "And it's way past that."

Her school lunch was a distant memory. Now the aroma of her dad's scrumptious lasagna was torturing her.

"Dinner is ready right now," he said. "But let's wait for Mom."

"For how long?" asked Amelia Bedelia. Her stomach growled.

"If she doesn't walk through the door in five minutes, we'll start without her. Deal?"

"Deal," said Amelia Bedelia.

They shook on it. Amelia Bedelia's stomach rumbled again.

"Honey, be a little patient!" said her father.

Amelia Bedelia's stomach answered, growling louder than ever.

"Daddy," said Amelia Bedelia, "if I don't eat soon, I'm going to be a little  patient in a big hospital." Her stomach rumbled again. "I'm really hungry."

Her father checked his watch. "Four minutes."

The month before, Amelia Bedelia's mother had been elected to the town council. Tonight was her first meeting.

To take her mind off her stomach, Amelia Bedelia asked a question she'd been wondering about.

"What does a treasurer do, anyway?" she asked. "Is Mom counting bags of gold and silver? Are there sacks of diamonds, emeralds, rubies, and . . . Is it as fun as it sounds?"

"I'm afraid not. It's more about numbers and balancing the books than about buried treasure," her father said.

"Don't be scared, Daddy," Amelia Bedelia said. "Mom will do a great job."

"She always does," said her father, checking his watch. "One more minute."

"How many books does

4

Mom have to balance?" asked Amelia Bedelia.

"Ask Mom," he said. "No matter what, your mother always comes through."

Just then the kitchen door swung open. "What will I come through?" asked Amelia Bedelia's mother.

"That door!" said Amelia Bedelia, running to give her mother a big hug.

"Family hug!" said Amelia Bedelia's

father, wrapping his arms around them. Even their dog, Finally, joined in—prancing and dancing and jumping around with excitement.

"Finally, off!" said Amelia Bedelia's mother, brushing down her pants. She was wearing a pantsuit and her fancy going-out shoes with the pointy toes.

"Don't you look smart today!" Amelia Bedelia's father said, giving her a kiss.

"Mom's smart every day!" said Amelia Bedelia.

"True," he said. "Amelia Bedelia and I were just saying that we're sure you'll do a great job on the town council," he explained to his wife.

"Thank you for your vote of confidence," said Amelia Bedelia's mother. Then she inhaled deeply to savor the aroma that filled their home.

"Mmmmm," she said. "Dinner smells fantastic. You're making my mouth water."

"Yuck!" Amelia Bedelia quickly handed her a paper towel.

YUCK!

"Let's eat!" said Amelia Bedelia's father. They said a super-fast grace so that Amelia Bedelia could dig in right away.

"So, tell us what happened at your first meeting," Amelia Bedelia's father continued.

"Well, there was some good news and some bad news," Amelia Bedelia's mother said.

"Let's hear the good news before the bad," said her father. "That makes the bad news easier to take."

"Well, a brand-new business is coming to town. An art supply store—"

"Yippee!" yelled Amelia Bedelia.

"I'm glad you came up for air," said her father. He handed Amelia Bedelia a piece of garlic bread, and she went back to eating.

"It will take a while," said Amelia Bedelia's mother. "The owners need lots of room and want the right space."

Amelia Bedelia's father scooped up a forkful of lasagna. "That is good news," he said. "What's the bad news?"

"It seems that people are recycling wrong," she said.

"How can it be wrong to recycle?" asked Amelia Bedelia.

"They're putting the wrong things into the bins," said her mother. "That contaminates everything, so *nothing* can be recycled. It all winds up at the landfill."

"That's terrible," said Amelia Bedelia.

"So give them a fine!" said Amelia Bedelia's father.

"You should not tell them it's fine when it's wrong," said Amelia Bedelia. "That would confuse people."

"Well, a fine was one suggestion," said Amelia Bedelia's mother. "But we're trying to come up with positive ideas to encourage folks to recycle correctly, instead of scaring them into it."

Amelia Bedelia's father nodded. "There's no need to twist anyone's arm," he said.

"Mom would never do something mean like that!" said Amelia Bedelia.

"Of course not," said her mother. "So,

guess who's in charge of coming up with ideas for how to fix this problem?"

Amelia Bedelia stared at her mother. "I give up. Who?"

"Yours truly!" said her mother.

"Mine truly?" asked Amelia Bedelia.

Her mother smiled, shaking her head. "Not you. Me!"

"Wow," said Amelia Bedelia's father. "Sounds like you really hit the ground running today."

Amelia Bedelia looked under the table at her mother's fancy footwear. "In *those* shoes?" she asked. "If you hit the ground running at your next meeting, you should wear sneakers!"

Chapter 2

Happy Hump Day to You!

"Morning, Daddy," said Amelia Bedelia as she walked into the kitchen the next morning.

Her father lowered the newspaper. "Happy Hump Day, Amelia Bedelia!" he said.

"What day?" said Amelia Bedelia.

"Hump Day," said her father.

"What hump?" said Amelia Bedelia. "Like a camel's hump? Is today National Camel Day? Or Take-Your-Local-Humpback-Whale-to-Lunch day?"

Her father was fond of inventing weird holidays and using them to tease her. "Which hump is it today?" said Amelia Bedelia. "Camel or whale?"

"Neither one," said her father. "Hump Day happens once a week. You may know it by another name. Some people call it Wednesday."

"Of course I've heard of Wednesday," said Amelia Bedelia.

"Well, Hump Day is Wednesday,"

said her father. "Week after week. Year in and year out.

Amelia Bedelia had heard of some weird holidays, but never one as silly as this. She looked straight into her father's eyes. "Daddy, are you making this up? It sounds too goofy, even for you."

Amelia Bedelia's mother closed the refrigerator with her hip, a jug of milk in one hand and a carton of eggs in the other. "It's true," she said. "Imagine riding your bike up a hill that gets steeper and steeper. In my office, that's what Monday and Tuesday feel like. At last you get to Wednesday and the middle of the week.

That day is
like the crest of a hill,
the hump. After Wednesday,
you can coast downhill to Thursday
and Friday, zooming into Saturday
and Sunday for a weekend to relax."

"Then it starts over again on Monday?"
asked Amelia Bedelia.

"I'm afraid so," said her father.

Hmmmm, thought Amelia Bedelia.
That was the second time her dad said
he was scared. She wondered why.

"Daddy and I came up with a fun idea
to celebrate Hump Day," said her mother.
"Every Wednesday we'll make waffles
for breakfast, because they start

with the letter *W*."

"Yum!" said Amelia Bedelia.

"Let's use toppings that start with the letter *W*, too!"

"Like whipped cream," said her mother.

"I love whipped cream!" said Amelia Bedelia.

"With walnuts on top," said her mother.

"You guys are hogging all the tasty toppings," said her father. "The only ones left that start with a *W* are . . . wasabi? Watercress? Worcestershire sauce?" He frowned.

"Ugh. I'm not hungry anymore," said Amelia Bedelia's mother.

While her father rummaged around

for tastier toppings, Amelia Bedelia and her mother got to work. They measured and mixed the ingredients while the waffle iron was getting hot. When it was ready, they poured in the batter and closed the top. Soon they had a stack of golden waffles staying warm in the oven.

Amelia Bedelia brought the waffles to the table. Her father put out all the toppings he had found. Besides whipped cream and walnuts, he had maple syrup, powdered sugar, all kinds of fresh  berries, fig jam, mini chocolate chips, and sprinkles for decorating cookies.

Amelia Bedelia put a waffle on

her plate, smothered it with toppings, then put another waffle on top. "Hey, I just invented the Topping Sandwich!" she said.

"Looks yummy," said her father. "While I was hunting for toppings, I remembered a joke about camels and humps."

"Why am I not surprised?" asked Amelia Bedelia's mother.

"Let's hear it, Daddy," said Amelia Bedelia.

"What do you call a camel without a hump?" he said.

Amelia Bedelia and her mother looked at each other and then back at him.

"A camel without a hump is a llama," said Amelia Bedelia's mother.

Amelia Bedelia and her mother giggled.

"No, a camel is still a camel, even without a hump," said her father. "Give up?"

Amelia Bedelia and her mother nodded.

"A camel without a hump is called Humphrey," said her father.

Amelia Bedelia and her mother looked at each other again, and back at him.

"Get it?" he said. "A camel without a hump is hump-free. It sounds like the name Humphrey. Get it? Hump? Free?"

"Yes, I got it," said Amelia Bedelia's mother. "Like a bad cold."

"Me, too," said Amelia Bedelia. "But I don't want it."

"Humph!" said her father

and went back to reading the newspaper. He began slowly shaking his head. "What is wrong with people in this town?" he asked.

Amelia Bedelia waited, expecting to hear a goofy punch line. Finally, she said, "I give up. What is wrong with the people in this town?"

Amelia Bedelia's father held up the paper and pointed to a picture and a headline. "This is no joke," he said.

Amelia Bedelia read the headline out loud. "THE WRITING IS ON THE WALL." Then she said, "What writing on what wall?"

"It's a play on words," said her mother.

"Like Humphrey and Hump-Free. Newspapers do that to attract your attention."

"'The writing is on the wall' is a saying," explained her father. "It means that it is obvious that something is about to happen—usually something bad. The writing on this wall is the graffiti that someone spray-painted on a wall in the park." He pointed at the picture on the front page. There were giant letters, taller than Amelia Bedelia, painted on the wall.

"What's so bad about that?" asked Amelia Bedelia. She kind of liked the artwork. "If the person who did this is an artist, isn't it okay for them to share their art? Doesn't everyone love art?"

"It's graffiti, though, cupcake," said Amelia Bedelia's mother. "If whoever painted it gets caught, something bad *will* happen—the graffiti artist will be in big trouble and probably get a fine."

There was that word again, thought Amelia Bedelia. Fine.

"Expressing yourself is fine," said her father. "Just don't do it on public property where everyone has to live with it and look at it whether they want to or not."

Amelia Bedelia sighed. This had been a busy Hump Day so far. And they weren't even at the top of the hill. She still had the rest of Wednesday to go. There certainly was a lot happening in her life: A new art supply store was opening. There were problems with recycling. Figuring out what was actually fine was not fine at all. She would have a lot to think about on her way to school.

School! She glanced at the clock just as her mother said, "Amelia Bedelia, you'll be late for school!"

Amelia Bedelia grabbed her backpack and kissed her mom and dad. "Do you know how vegetables say goodbye?" she asked.

"No," said her father.

"How?" asked her mother.

"Peas out!" said Amelia Bedelia as she headed out the door.

Chapter 3

Fish Fingers and Swing Hogs

When Amelia Bedelia arrived at school, her teacher and some of her friends were busily arranging the chairs into a circle in the middle of the room. *Oh no!* thought Amelia Bedelia. She had forgotten that they were having morning meeting today. She felt bad that she wasn't prepared to share something.

After the kids sat down, Mrs. Shauk took her place in the circle, making it look like a flat tire. "Welcome to morning meeting," she said to the class. "Now, who wants to get the ball rolling?"

Amelia Bedelia laughed. She almost blurted out, *This isn't gym class, Mrs. Shauk!*

"Don't be shy," said Mrs. Shauk. "Who would like to go first?"

25

Skip raised his hand. "I will," he said. "It's about the fifth graders. They won't let us use the swings during recess."

"Well, that doesn't sound fair," said Mrs. Shauk. "Anyone have any ideas about how we could fix this?"

"How about time limits?" said Roger. "The fifth graders get the swings for the first half of recess, and we get the swings for the second half."

"Good suggestion," said Mrs. Shauk. "Now, who wants to watch the clock?"

Amelia Bedelia didn't think anyone would volunteer for that. And she was right.

Penny raised her hand. "My sister is in the fifth grade, and she says the only reason they are on the swings so much is because our class hogs the foursquare court."

"Is that true?" asked Mrs. Shauk.

"Only because they hog the swings!" said Clay.

The class began to buzz. Amelia Bedelia thought it sounded like a beehive had been stirred up. She glanced at Penny and Clay. She wondered when pigs had gotten onto the playground.

Just then, Joy spoke up. "Can't Mr. Jack paint more foursquare courts?" Mr. Jack was their school handyman. He could fix anything.

Mrs. Shauk nodded. "What a simple solution! I'll bring it up with Principal Hotchkiss. Anyone else?"

Heather raised her hand. "There's a really big problem in the cafeteria," she said. "We haven't had pizza for over two weeks!"

Everyone agreed this was a problem. Kids who ate school lunch really looked forward to pizza day.

"And even worse, they've been serving fish fingers instead," continued Holly.

Amelia Bedelia shuddered. Did fish actually have fingers, or were those fins? "Gross!" she said. What would be next in

28

the cafeteria? Fish gills? Fish eyeballs?

"That does not sound like an equal substitution," said Mrs. Shauk. "Maybe there is a reason in the kitchen that we don't know about. I'll ask Mrs. Roman and keep you posted."

Wade went next. He was pretty upset. "Why was I the only one in the whole class not invited to Teddy's birthday party?"

"That's impossible," said Teddy. "I invited everyone."

"Then where is my invitation?" asked Skip.

"We emailed them," Teddy explained. "My mom says that paper invitations just end up in the recycling bin."

Recycling—that's it! Amelia Bedelia suddenly remembered that she *did* have something to share after all.

"Great work today, class," said Mrs. Shauk. "Now let's all return our chairs to—"

Amelia Bedelia raised her hand and waved it around. "Um, can we wait a second, please? I have something to share," she said. "I just found out that people are putting things that can't be recycled into their recycling bins. The recyclables get contaminated and have to be thrown into the garbage. Does anyone have any ideas to fix this?"

"My goodness!" Mrs. Shauk

said. "What disappointing news. I take my recycling very seriously. I even recycle the tiny paper tags from my tea bags!"

Chip raised his hand. "I help my grandma with her recycling," he said. "Otherwise she would put in things that don't belong!"

"It's super confusing," said Pat. "Your grandma could use a chart."

"A chart would be perfect!" said Amelia Bedelia. "Let's design a really cool one and make copies!"

"On recycled paper, of course," Chip added. "We could hand them out this weekend."

Clay groaned. "This weekend? That's when Cliff and I are riding bikes."

Suddenly Amelia Bedelia had an idea. Not a big idea, sort of a medium one. "We can combine the two! We can make signs about recycling and decorate our bikes and ride around handing out the flyers."

Clay shrugged. "Sure, why not?"

"We can even ride to the park!" said Rose. "The farmers' market is Saturday. Lots of people will be there."

"What great teamwork!" said Mrs. Shauk. "I'll send a note to your parents. Let's meet here at school on Saturday morning and then ride over together. You can start making signs and decorations during recess!"

"We will be Cycling for Recycling!" said Amelia Bedelia. She looked around the circle at her friends with a big smile on her face. Her mom was going to be thrilled when she told her about the plan.

"Amelia Bedelia, you look like the cat that ate the canary!" said Mrs. Shauk.

Amelia Bedelia's eyes widened. *Was that a compliment?* she wondered. She loved cats and would never eat a canary. The more she thought about it, the wider her eyes got. "Thank you, I guess?" she said.

Chapter 4

Birds of a Feather Flock Shauk Together

"Hey, Amelia Bedelia!" Cliff shouted. "Look at me!"

Amelia Bedelia and her friends were milling about in front of Oak Tree

Elementary on Saturday morning. They were putting the finishing touches on their bicycles and adjusting their helmets. Cliff had glued several aluminum cans on his helmet. He also wore a long blue cape with a big white R on it. "I'm Recycling Man!" he cried.

"You look so cool, Cliff," said Amelia Bedelia.

"I can't believe you guys pulled this off, and so quickly!" said Amelia Bedelia's mother.

Dawn came running up. "Mrs. Shauk just got here, and she is going to knock your socks off!"

Amelia Bedelia checked her feet. Her sneakers were double-knotted. "Impossible," she said.

"Come with me," said Dawn, pulling Amelia Bedelia through the crowd. And there was Mrs. Shauk, sitting on the front seat of a bicycle built for two. With another Mrs. Shauk on the back seat!

"Good morning, Amelia Bedelia," said Mrs. Shauk. "Allow me to introduce you to my twin sister, Mrs. Regal."

Amelia Bedelia knew it was rude, but she couldn't help it. She just stared with her mouth open.

"Salutations, Amelia Bedelia," said Mrs. Regal.

"So you're the one who spearheaded Cycling for Recycling."

"Yes, that's me," said Amelia Bedelia.

"Well, bravo. Well done!" said Mrs. Regal.

"Thank you," said Amelia Bedelia.

Mrs. Regal's hair was a bit longer than Mrs. Shauk's. And her glasses were a different color. But other than that, they were identical, right down to their matching pointy red fingernails.

Then, without warning or turning around, Mrs. Regal demanded, "Young man, where is your helmet?"

Behind her, Wade looked up, eyes wide. "I'll go get it," he said.

Clay nudged Amelia Bedelia.

37

"Mrs. Shauk's sister has the same sharp eyes," he said.

"Oh, great," whispered Cliff.

"Shauk the Hawk meets Regal the Eagle. We can barely handle one of them, and now there are two!" Amelia Bedelia stifled a laugh.

Mrs. Shauk addressed the group. "Thank you all for participating in Cycling for Recycling! And thank you, Amelia Bedelia, for bringing this issue to our

attention. We'll ride to the park together, make a big loop, and hand out the flyers to everyone we see. Now let's hit the road!"

Everyone cheered as Amelia Bedelia, leading the pack, pedaled toward the park. She certainly did not want to hit the road. She had fallen off her bike once, a long time ago. She had hit the road very hard and was not looking for a repeat experience.

It was a beautiful day. The sun warmed Amelia Bedelia's shoulders while a pleasant breeze brushed her face. Just ahead was a flash of color. Amelia Bedelia steered over to the curb and stopped to get a closer look. It was just a mailbox, but it looked amazing. It had been transformed into a work of art. Brightly colored bubble letters on the side spelled out SAS. Amelia Bedelia knew that she was not supposed to like it, but she could not help herself.

Mrs. Shauk pulled up beside her. "I hope they put a stop to this graffiti," she said. "Look how someone has defaced this mailbox!"

"Defaced?" said Amelia Bedelia. She was pretty sure that their mailbox at home did not have a face. She wondered

what the face of a mailbox would look like. And where had this mailbox's face gone?

"Let's get going," said Mrs. Shauk. "Everyone is ahead of us now."

Amelia Bedelia did not mind that at all. She began to sing softly under her breath. She had stayed up late the night before, working on a special song about recycling. She began to sing louder, to the tune of "I've Been Working on the Railroad."

It's important to recycle!
Recycling is great.
It's important to recycle
But do it wrong—you'll contaminate!
So please be really, really careful

And do your neighbors proud.
We really shouldn't have to say this
But no diapers are allowed!

"Great song, Amelia Bedelia!" shouted Mrs. Shauk. Or was it Mrs. Regal?

On Monday morning, Mrs. Shauk asked the class for feedback at the morning meeting. "Amelia Bedelia, do you have anything to report back to us about Cycling for Recycling?"

"My mom said it was a huge success," Amelia Bedelia told everyone. "The only problem is that we didn't make nearly enough flyers. People have been calling the city hall for more copies!"

"Sounds like a happy problem," said Mrs. Shauk.

"There is one other problem," said Amelia Bedelia slowly. "When people found out there were things they couldn't recycle, they didn't want to just throw them out, and they filled the donation table at the recycling center. Now the town council has no idea what to do with all that stuff!"

Mrs. Shauk had a thoughtful look on her face. But all she said was, "Very interesting."

Chapter 5

From Trash to Treasure

The next morning at exactly ten a.m., Mrs. Shauk clapped her hands. "Attention, class!" she said. "A special guest is here to visit us today. Let's head outside to meet her. Please line up quietly. I don't want to hear a peep."

Amelia Bedelia didn't know about her friends, but she

44

hadn't been planning on peeping.
That was strictly for the birds. But Clay
obviously couldn't resist. Walking behind
Amelia Bedelia, he kept saying, "Peep!
Peep! Peep!"

Mrs. Shauk led the students outside.
Sitting on their tree stump, which
doubled as a student lounge, was their
special guest, a young woman with long,
straight brown hair that fell to her waist.
She wore paint-speckled overalls with a
striped T-shirt and clogs on her feet. She

was surrounded by several large, brightly colored works of art.

Their guest smiled when she saw them. It was one of the happiest smiles Amelia Bedelia had ever seen. "Elsie!" the young woman cried. She ran over to Mrs. Shauk and threw her arms around her. Amelia Bedelia and her friends watched in disbelief as she lifted Mrs. Shauk right off the ground in a giant bear hug.

"Mrs. Shauk's name is Elsie?" said Dawn. That was surprising. And even more shocking, Mrs. Shauk wasn't mad about being picked up like a baby—she was laughing.

"Class," Mrs. Shauk

said breathlessly, "let me introduce you to Jackie, my dear friend's daughter. I'll let her tell you all about her wonderful art, and then you'll understand why I asked her here today."

Amelia Bedelia took a closer look at the sculptures next to the stump. There was an alligator with a wide-open mouth full of pointy teeth, ready to snap. A flamingo preened its bright pink feathers as it gracefully balanced itself on one thin leg. A yellow dog rolled on its back, its red tongue lolling out of its mouth. A monkey, eating a banana, hung by its tail from a tree branch.

"Go ahead, touch them!" Jackie said. "You're allowed! You can even smell them if you want! You won't be the first!" She threw her head back and laughed. It was a deep belly laugh, and you couldn't help but smile when you heard it.

Amelia Bedelia and her friends stepped forward and examined the artwork. It wasn't often that you were allowed to touch art, let alone smell it. Amelia Bedelia poked at the monkey, and it swung back and forth. The sculptures were made out of a colorful translucent material, sturdily held together with bits and pieces of wire. They were fun, bright, and quite beautiful. They glowed like stained glass when the sunlight hit them.

"Can anyone guess what my sculptures are made out of?" Jackie asked.

"Glass?" offered Holly.

"Close, but no cigar," said Jackie.

Amelia Bedelia wrinkled her nose. Thank goodness. Cigars smelled terrible.

"Is it . . . plastic?" Joy guessed.

"Yes! My sculptures are made of plastic bottles that I cut up and fastened together with wire," Jackie explained. "I am a recycled-materials artist. I make art out of garbage!"

"Wow!" said Daisy. "I had no

idea garbage could be so beautiful."

"Thank you kindly," said Jackie with a deep bow. She straightened up. "Now, please sit down and get comfortable!" She pointed to a large tarp spread out on the grass. "As we all know, it is very important to recycle. But did you know that there are different ways to do it?" She reached into her backpack and pulled out a bottle. "Now the usual way to recycle a glass bottle like this is to sort, wash, crush, melt, and mold it into a new shape. It's a long process called downcycling. Can anyone guess what my type of recycling is called?"

"Upcycling?" Pat guessed.

"You got it!" cried Jackie. "Now, I

have a friend who takes these very same bottles and upcycles them into drinking glasses. He cuts them, polishes the edges, and etches designs onto them. The bottles don't need to be broken down, so it saves energy." She tapped the bottle. "All types of recycling are good, because they result in less landfill. But as you can see, I prefer upcycling."

"Why do you use plastic in your art?" Pat asked.

"Plastic is suffocating our planet," Jackie explained. "Did you know that Americans use roughly thirty-five million plastic bottles and a hundred

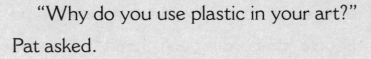

35,000,000

100,000,000,000

billion plastic bags a year?"

Amelia Bedelia and her friends gasped.

"It's true," said Jackie. "The amount of plastic thrown out in one year could circle our planet four times," she said. "And it can take a thousand years for plastic to decompose.

"Ever since I was a little girl, I've had a passion for the environment. It makes me so happy to turn things that people don't want anymore into beautiful, useful new things." She smiled. "My sculptures show people that you don't need expensive materials to create art. You can literally make art out of anything, even garbage."

Jackie picked up a duffel bag and flipped it over. A cascade of empty plastic water bottles flowed onto the tarp she had spread out.

"Today you are going to make your very own sculptures out of garbage. Or as I like to call it, trash treasure." She and Mrs. Shauk began handing out safety scissors, pipe cleaners, hole punches, and multicolored permanent markers to Amelia Bedelia and her friends.

"It's easy! Decide what you want to create, cut up the bottles with the scissors, and color the pieces any way you like. Then fasten the pieces together. Can anyone guess how?" Jackie asked.

"With glue?" suggested Holly.

Jackie pointed to her overalls.

"Think sturdier, like clothing," she said.

"We're going to *sew* them?" asked Heather.

"Exactly!" said Jackie. "Clothing needs to be durable, and so does our art. So we are going to make holes in the plastic pieces with hole punches, and then stitch them together with pipe cleaners. Are you ready to make some art?"

Everyone started grabbing plastic bottles.

"Don't forget—safety first!" said Jackie. "Always be careful when using any tools!"

"I'm going to make a grasshopper," said Teddy, selecting a bright green marker.

Clay and Cliff decided they would both make horses.

"I think you all know what I'm going to make," said Mrs. Shauk.

"A hawk!" the class chorused.

"That's right," Mrs. Shauk said with a smile. She sat cross-legged on the tarp and picked up a pair of safety scissors.

Amelia Bedelia decided she'd make an armadillo.

"Jackie," Mrs. Shauk said, once everyone had a good

start on their projects. "There's another reason I brought you here. It seems that our town has an overabundance of stuff that is too good to throw away but can't be recycled."

Jackie's eyes lit up. "Too much trash treasure? That sounds spifftacular!" she said.

"Spifftacular?" said Joy, looking up from her lizard. "Is that a word?"

"It is now," said Clay.

Mrs. Shauk agreed. "Ever since she was a little girl, Jackie has liked to make up new words, by combining old words."

"It's true," said Jackie. "I upcycle everything. Even words!" She smiled. "And your news *is* spifftacular. I'm always on the lookout for materials."

"Are you going to upcycle all the town's extra garbage?" asked Penny. "Cool! I love that idea."

"Join the club!" said Jackie. "I love it too!"

Amelia Bedelia looked up from her armadillo.

"Is it an art club?" she asked

Jackie squinted at Amelia Bedelia. "No, I meant . . ." Then she thought for

a minute. "An art club is a wonderful idea! I can give upcycling lessons at my studio with all the new trash treasure! I'm almost done with the pieces for my art show anyway," she said. "We could call it the Upcycling Art Club!"

Mrs. Shauk looked over at Amelia Bedelia. "Nice work," she said. Amelia Bedelia wasn't sure if the Hawk meant her armadillo (which was super cute) or her art-club idea. Maybe both, she figured.

Too soon, Mrs. Shauk said, "Time's up! Let's get to science class."

Amelia Bedelia and her friends groaned good-naturedly. Then they clustered around Jackie to show off their creations.

"Hold your horses!" said Ms. Shauk.

Amelia Bedelia pointed to Cliff and Clay. "They are!" she said. "And we're holding our snakes, lizards, armadillos, unicorns, monkeys, bunnies, dragons, and bumblebees too," she added.

"We were so excited about our animals we forgot to say thank you!" said Mrs. Shauk.

"Thank you, Jackie," the class chorused.

"Thank *you*," said Jackie. "What a creative bunch you are. You guys are all fantabulous artists!"

As Amelia Bedelia and her friends headed back inside, Jackie started packing up. She hoisted the alligator over her shoulder and waved merrily to the class.

"See you later, alligators!" she called.

"After a while, crocodile!" everyone shouted back.

Amelia Bedelia and her friends could hear Jackie's deep, delighted laugh all the way back to their classroom.

Chapter 6

New Club, Old Friend

"Look here, that graffiti gang has struck again!" said Amelia Bedelia's father. He held up the newspaper at breakfast on Saturday morning.

Amelia Bedelia shut the dishwasher door and turned around. "What did they hit? I thought they just painted things."

"This time they tagged the old paint factory on Industrial Road." He shook his head. "Not that it makes a difference anyway. That old place is such an eyesore."

"That building is supposed to be demolished anyway," said Amelia Bedelia's mother. "People think it's old and ugly. Nobody wants to look at it anymore."

"We'll all be glad to see it go," said Amelia Bedelia's father.

"I won't," said her mother. "That factory played a huge part in this town for a really long time. You didn't grow up here, so it's hard for you to understand." She turned to Amelia Bedelia. "My

great-grandpa worked there. Employees got a discount on paint, and he painted every room in his house a different color! I used to love visiting his house."

She sighed and stood up from the breakfast table. "Ready, sweetie?" she asked. "Before we go, let's check our attic and see if we can find any more things to upcycle."

"Jackie picked up all that stuff from the recycling center," said Amelia Bedelia. "She probably doesn't need anything else."

"I've been meaning to clean out the attic for months now," said her mother. "Let's look. Humor me."

"Okay," said Amelia Bedelia. "You know what you call someone who loves their attic?" she said as they headed upstairs.

"I don't know," said Amelia Bedelia's mother. "What *do* you call someone who loves their attic?" she said.

"A fan-attic!" replied Amelia Bedelia.

Amelia Bedelia's mother groaned. "That joke has been recycled so many times."

An hour later Amelia Bedelia was finally on her way to upcycling club. She was pulling an overstuffed wagon behind her, full of trash treasure. She had a

dressmaker's dummy. Several lamps. An old-fashioned wire birdcage. A bag of costume jewelry needing repair. A dented metal ceiling light in a color that could only be described as goose-poop green.

It was still early, so Amelia Bedelia took a detour. She wanted to check out the latest graffiti. She didn't care what anyone said. To her, it was pretty.

Amelia Bedelia headed down Maple Street and made a left onto Industrial Road. She walked for a while until

she came to a stop in front of the old abandoned building. She tried to imagine her great-great-grandfather arriving at work, swinging his lunch box, waving hello to his fellow workers.

But now it was hard to picture this sad, forgotten building filled with life. Its gray walls were dull and dingy, and the glass left in the broken windows looked like jagged monster teeth. Turning the

corner, Amelia Bedelia glimpsed a flash
of color. Graffiti! This time the tag was
much bigger, with flowers that were
beautiful and intricate.

"Wow," she said.

A teenage girl, the ends of her blond

hair dyed bright blue, stood nearby.
"Yeah?" she said. "Do you want to
make something of it?"

"No thanks. I'm making stuff out

of this," said Amelia Bedelia, pointing to her wagon.

"That garbage?" scoffed the girl.

"It's not garbage," said Amelia Bedelia. "It's trash treasure!"

The girl walked over. "Huh?" she said. "What did you say? I think our wires are crossed."

Amelia Bedelia looked down at her wagon and shook her head. "Nope. My wires are all in the wagon," she said. She tried again. "This is future upcycled art."

"*What* cycled?" said the girl.

So Amelia Bedelia explained.

"That's pretty cool," the girl said. "Turning something old and forgotten into something beautiful." She pointed

to the graffiti. "Like this."

"Exactly," said Amelia Bedelia. "That's really . . . spifftacular."

"I like that," the girl said. "It really *is* spifftacular, isn't it?" She took one last look at the wall and nodded. "Later," said the girl over her shoulder as she walked away.

"Bye," said Amelia Bedelia.

When Amelia Bedelia arrived at the studio, a bunch of kids were waiting outside. Cliff, Clay, Dawn, and Daisy were there. There were also some kids she didn't recognize, probably from another school . . . and . . .

"Alice, is that you?" Amelia Bedelia said in disbelief. She dropped the handle of her wagon and ran over to hug her friend. It was Alice from Camp Echo Woods! Alice went to school on the other side of town, and Amelia Bedelia didn't get to see her very often. "You're joining this club too?"

"You bet I am," said Alice, squeezing Amelia Bedelia's arm. "I haven't seen you in forever and a day!"

"That's impossible!" said Amelia Bedelia.

70

"But it has been a super long time."

"These are my friends from school," said Alice. She introduced Amelia Bedelia to her friends. "This is my camp buddy, Amelia Bedelia," she told them. "She's an old friend."

"Actually, we're the exact same age," said Amelia Bedelia.

"Amelia Bedelia, we've heard so much about you!" said one of Alice's friends.

71

"And these are my friends Cliff, Clay,
Daisy, and Dawn," said Amelia Bedelia.

"Yoo-hoo! Helloppy!" called a familiar
voice. Everyone spun around. And there
was Jackie, riding up on a bicycle. She was
wearing a big pair of yellow sunglasses and
a large straw hat festooned with flowers.
A tiny white dog sat in the basket. It too
wore a hat and sunglasses.

"This is my dog, Debris," Jackie said.
Debris stood up in the basket and wagged

his tail. "He comes with me to the studio every day."

Amelia Bedelia stared at Jackie's bicycle. It looked more like a collage of a bicycle than an actual one. It was like nothing she had ever seen before.

"I call it my re-cycle!" Jackie said. "It's made of discarded bicycle parts. I collected them one by one and put them together. Isn't it wonderiferous?"

Jackie unlocked the studio door, and the students filed in.

"Wow," said Amelia Bedelia. The studio was an open room with high ceilings and a large skylight. Jackie's sculptures hung from the walls and the ceiling. Amelia Bedelia recognized some and also spotted a few new ones—a crab, an octopus, a lion with a multicolored mane. When the sunlight hit the sculptures, the white walls were dappled with rainbow rays of light.

There was a large worktable in the middle of the room. The walls were lined with bins filled with art supplies and jumbled piles of the things Jackie had collected from the recycling center.

Alice leaned over to whisper in Amelia Bedelia's ear. "Imagine if Mrs. Evans came here. She hates litter so much. She'd really flip her lid." Mrs. Evans was the owner of Camp Echo Woods, where Alice had met Amelia Bedelia.

"And she'd go crazy too," said Amelia
Bedelia. She turned to Jackie. "This is
so amazing," she said. "I hope you have
room for some more stuff."

Jackie's eyes lit up when she saw the
contents of Amelia Bedelia's wagon.
"There's always room for more!" she
said. "I love it all! And this could really

be the bee's knees," she said, pointing at the drab ceiling light.

"Cute and fuzzy?" Amelia Bedelia guessed.

"Anything you want it to be!" replied Jackie.

Everyone took a seat around the table. "Welcome to upcycling class and my art studio!" said Jackie. "The club will officially meet on Saturday mornings, but the studio will be open every afternoon after school too. You are free to create anything you like with the materials here. And I'll be around to help you with whatever you may need!"

The kids started rooting through the

piles of stuff, holding up objects and waiting to be inspired. Alice, who had just gotten a new puppy, decided to  take a bunch of vitamin jars with lids that popped open and some wallpaper samples and make a set of puppy-treat dispensers. "Perfect for training," she said. Cliff found an old mirror and some toy alphabet blocks. He was going to arrange the blocks into a frame around the mirror, spelling a message.

Clay started sorting through a pile. "Hey, why is garbage so sad?" he asked.

"Why?" said Dawn.

"Because it's down in the dumps!"

"Not our trash treasure!" said Alice. "It's happy to be here."

"That's because our trash treasure is here with us," said Amelia Bedelia. "And we are making it into something special."

Jackie came over and dumped an armload of old T-shirts on the table. "I scooped up a ton of these at the recycling center," she said.

Amelia Bedelia's eyes widened. "Wow!" she said. "You must be really strong."

"Why, yes, I am," said Jackie, flexing her arm.

Amelia Bedelia picked up one of the T-shirts, trying to figure out what she could make. Then she remembered what Jackie had said about plastic bags. Could she turn an old T-shirt into a tote bag? She could cut off the sleeves and make shoulder straps. But how would she seal up the bottom? Amelia Bedelia was not much of a sewer. But after some trial and error she figured out how to do it without a needle and thread. She turned the shirt inside out, cut strips along the bottom of the T-shirt, and knotted them together.

"Holy reusable tote bags!" said Jackie when she saw Amelia Bedelia's handiwork. "What a fantasmical idea!"

"Do you think we could make enough of these so the whole town could stop using plastic bags?" asked Amelia Bedelia.

"That's a lot of T-shirts, so it might be hard," said Jackie. "But the word *never* isn't in my vocabulary!"

Amelia Bedelia stared at Jackie. "Are you sure about that?" she asked.

"Sure about what?" asked Jackie.

"That the word *never* is not in your vocabulary. Because you just said it."

Jackie smiled. "It really isn't. I never take no for an answer!"

"See, you said it again!" said Amelia Bedelia. "So it *is* in your vocabulary!"

"Nope!" Jackie said cheerfully, shaking her head at the same time.

Amelia Bedelia shrugged and selected another T-shirt. She had more important things to think about—like getting rid of plastic bags in her town, one tote at a time!

Chapter Seven

A Miner Detail

"Can you guys believe it?" asked Heather on Monday morning. "The graffiti artist was caught in the act last night." Heather's aunt was a police officer, so she often had the latest scoop on what was going on in town.

"What a talented person," said Amelia Bedelia. "Imagine being a graffiti artist and an actor too. That's amazing."

"You didn't hear this from me, Amelia Bedelia, but the artist is a minor. They will only have to do some community service," whispered Heather.

Amelia Bedelia gave her friend a funny look.

"But I did hear you say it," she said. "Plus, why does a miner get treated better than anyone else? Did they strike gold or discover diamonds?

Heather shrugged. "Minors always get off easier," she said. "Because they're minors."

"Well, that doesn't sound fair," said Amelia Bedelia.

She planned to bring it up at their next morning meeting.

After school, Amelia Bedelia headed to Jackie's studio to meet Alice. She was on her twenty-fourth tote bag. She also made some cool pushpins and magnets.

"I'm so excited you're coming over for dinner tonight," she told Alice. "I asked my mom to make your favorite camp meal—mac and cheese with cut-up hot dogs."

"Yum!" said Alice. "Now if we could only make s'mores and sing songs by the campfire, it would be perfect!" She held up a finished placemat. She had figured

s'mores!

out how to upcycle plastic bags by cutting them into strips, braiding them, and then sewing them into coasters, placemats, and bowls. "What do you think?

"Wow!" said Amelia Bedelia. "You're so good at that!" She turned to Jackie. "Do you think that maybe we could sell our upcycling at your art show? That way we could make money to buy art supplies, so you don't have to buy everything."

"What an amazetastic idea!" said Jackie. "Amelia Bedelia, you are always thinking!"

"Yes, I am," said Amelia Bedelia. Even when she was sleeping, her brain was still working. Ms. Garcia had taught her that in science class.

"My show is in two weeks," said Jackie. She sighed. "I wish more people were coming. The last time I checked, only six people had said they would come. And that includes my grandma, my parents, and Elsie."

After they were finished at the studio, Amelia Bedelia and Alice took the long way home. Amelia Bedelia wanted to see the latest (and likely the last) graffiti.

"Ooh, it's pretty," said Alice, looking up at the abandoned building. "I like the colors. And the flowers."

"No, that's the old one," said Amelia Bedelia. "I wonder where the new one could be. . . ." She spun around and spotted an archway she hadn't seen before. "Come on!" she said to Alice.

Amelia Bedelia and Alice tiptoed through the archway and into a large open courtyard. Weeds grew through cracks in the cement. There were a few knocked-over planters and some weather-beaten benches. It was amazing.

But where was the graffiti?

Then Amelia Bedelia spotted it. But it was only halfway done. It ended abruptly, with a squiggle of pink paint.

"Looks like the graffiti artist was caught red-handed," said Alice.

"More like pink-handed," said Amelia Bedelia.

"Oh good, you're here," said Amelia Bedelia's mother when she and Alice arrived home. "We've got to eat quickly. There's an emergency town council meeting tonight, and Daddy has to work late. You can stay with Mrs. Adams next

door while I drop Alice at her house on my way to town hall."

Amelia Bedelia looked at Alice. She whispered in her ear. Alice nodded.

"We'd like to come to the meeting," said Amelia Bedelia.

"Really?" said her mother. "You might be bored to tears."

"We're not crybabies, Mom!" said Amelia Bedelia.

WAAAAA!!

"Of course you're not," said her mother. "I just meant that . . ." She looked at the girls, who gazed back at her hopefully. "Okay, but brace yourselves!"

Amelia Bedelia and Alice took their seats. The town hall was packed! Amelia Bedelia felt very proud to see her mother sitting at the long table in front of the room with the rest of the town council.

The mayor stood up. He wore a yellow-and-green bow tie and a yellow pocket square. Amelia Bedelia took a quick peek at his socks. *Yes!* They were bright green. She wondered if he wore different matching colors every day of the week.

"I move that we call this meeting to order," the mayor said, lifting a pile of paper into the air and waving it around. "Do we have a motion to waive the reading of the minutes from our last meeting?" He looked out at the audience expectantly.

Amelia Bedelia raised her hand. She waved at the mayor like he had asked.

"Do we have a second?" said the mayor.

A lady sitting in the front row raised her hand.

"All in favor of waiving the reading and approving the minutes of last month's meeting, say aye."

"Say I what?" whispered Amelia Bedelia to Alice.

"I don't know," said Alice.

"Aye," said the crowd.

"All against, say nay," said the mayor. There was silence.

Say *neigh*? Amelia Bedelia

looked around. She wondered what was going on. They wouldn't be expecting any neighs if they didn't have any horses. She figured that if they could have pigs on their playground, they might have horses at the town council.

"No nays, so the motion has passed," said the mayor.

Alice turned to Amelia Bedelia. "This is pretty boring so far!" she whispered. "If the whole meeting is like this, I think I *am* going to cry!"

Next it was time to review the budget. Amelia Bedelia tried to concentrate as her mother explained it, line by line. But words like *fiscal*, *capital improvements*, and *unencumbered balances* were making her eyes feel heavy. She hoped some horses would show up now. She and Alice would ride them home. She even started to wish she had stayed with Mrs. Adams, even though Mrs. Adams was a million years old. At least they could have baked brownies or something.

"The next order of business is to vote on the community service for our graffiti artist," said the mayor. "The town records department has a job in mind, filing papers for thirty days. All in favor, say . . ."

Amelia Bedelia jumped up. "I—"

"Why, thank you, Amelia Bedelia," said the mayor, cutting her off. "Is everyone else in favor?"

"I . . . I . . . I . . . ," sputtered Amelia Bedelia.

"I'm sorry, but you only get one vote," said the mayor.

"I am trying to say that I have a different idea! A big idea!" Amelia Bedelia exclaimed.

Everyone turned to stare at Amelia Bedelia. She could feel her face getting warm. Alice began to sink down in her

seat. Even Amelia Bedelia's mother, at the head table, was beginning to blush.

"The town council recognizes Amelia Bedelia," said the mayor.

"This is so weird," Amelia Bedelia whispered to Alice. "Of course they recognize me! Especially Mom!"

"Tell them your idea, Amelia Bedelia," whispered Alice.

"My idea is that that the graffiti artist do her community service at the

Upcycling Art Studio," said Amelia Bedelia. "We take the trash treasures from the recycling center and upcycle them into cool and useful things. But there's a ton of trash, and we could use some help!"

"Well said, Amelia Bedelia," said the mayor. "And an excellent suggestion. I do believe we should take a vote. All in favor of the graffiti artist doing her community service at the Upcycling Art Studio, say aye."

There was a loud chorus of ayes. The sound echoed around the room. Amelia Bedelia couldn't believe it. She gave Alice a high five and waved at the mayor.

"The ayes have it!" said the mayor. "Now, next on the agenda is the fate of

the old paint factory on Industrial Road."
He looked at his watch. "But it's getting
late. I move to table the discussion until
our next meeting. That old eyesore isn't
going anywhere, that's for sure. Do I
have a motion to close the meeting?"

Amelia Bedelia stood up again. "I'd
like to, uh, put it on the table that the
Upcycling Art Studio is having an art
show of splendiferous upcycled art and
goods in two weeks! You can tell
us you're coming at the website."

"Anyone want to second that motion?"
said the mayor.

"I second and third it!" said Alice.

The mayor laughed. "Duly noted. And
may I add that this meeting is certainly

more interesting when you and your friends are here, Amelia Bedelia."

With that, the meeting was adjourned.

Alice jumped up and gave Amelia Bedelia a huge hug. "You were great!"

Amelia Bedelia's mother hugged both Amelia Bedelia and Alice, saying, "I'm so proud of you I could burst!"

Amelia Bedelia was alarmed. "Don't do that, Mom!"

Chapter 8

Ophelia ~~Amelia~~ Bedelia?

"Amelia Bedelia, you made the paper this morning!" her father exclaimed when Amelia Bedelia came down for breakfast the next morning.

"Nope. The only thing I made was my bed," said Amelia Bedelia, grabbing a piece of toast.

"And the front page,

to boot!" said her father, holding up the paper.

"I wasn't wearing boots yesterday," said Amelia Bedelia. Her father ignored her and began reading from the article.

"Listen to this," he said. "'A local Oak Tree Elementary student interrupted the proceedings to suggest an alternative community service idea to the town council. Miss Ophelia Bedelia suggested— '"

"Who?" said Amelia Bedelia. "You

Ophelia?

see, that wasn't me. It was Ophelia."

Her father shrugged. "A minor detail," he said.

"But I'm not a miner, either," she said.

Her father kept on reading. "'The ayes had it, so the graffiti artist will be volunteering at the Upcycling Art Studio, turning this town's refuse into works of art.'"

"That's right," said Amelia Bedelia. "We don't refuse any refuse."

"I'm so proud of you, cupcake," said Amelia Bedelia's mother.

"Me too, muffin," said her father.

"Cupcake? Muffin?" said Amelia Bedelia. "Was I born or baked?"

Her parents hugged her from each side. "Family hug," said Amelia Bedelia. "Does it say anything about the show?"

Her father scanned the article. "Yes!

At the end. It gives the date and time and everything. Nice work! Hopefully your upcycling projects will sell like hotcakes."

"Dad, we are not serving breakfast at the show," Amelia Bedelia said. "Hotcakes or cold."

"Whatever you say, Ophelia Bedelia," said her father.

"Yipes!" exclaimed Jackie after checking the studio's website. "Now two hundred and twenty-eight people are coming to our show. Where are we going to put everyone? There's not enough room in here to swing a cat!"

"Why would you want

to do that?' asked Amelia Bedelia, her eyes wide. "What about the poor cat?"

Jackie plopped down in a chair at the table. Debris jumped into her lap. "What are we going to do?" Jackie asked. "We just have too many trash treasures!"

"Um, hello," called a voice. "You guys

look down in the dumps. Is this an art studio or what?"

Amelia Bedelia spun around. She was surprised to see the blue-haired girl she'd met at the old factory standing in the doorway. "This is an art studio, of course! And we've already been to the dump."

"I'm here to do my community service," said the girl.

"*You're* the graffiti artist?" Amelia Bedelia exclaimed.

"I am," said the girl. "My name is Olivia. And I wanted to thank whoever saved me from thirty days of filing papers in the town records department. This is way better!"

Jackie stood up and introduced herself. "You have Amelia Bedelia to thank," she said, pointing to her.

Olivia eyes narrowed. "I know you!" she said. "You liked my graffiti. You're the girl with the wagon full of garbage."

"Trash treasures," said the whole club in unison.

"That's what we call garbage here," explained Jackie. "Well, let's get you started. How about helping us with all the new stuff? I usually sort it by material. Paper, electronics, rubber,

paper

electronics

rubber
wood
plastic

wood, plastic, and so on."

"Sounds smart," said Olivia.

"Hey, what does a pirate steal in his spare time?" asked Clay.

Olivia looked up from her sorting.

"I don't know. What?" she said.

"Arrrrrrrrrrrrrt!" said Clay.

Arrrrrrrrrt!

"That's pretty good," Olivia said. "You got another one?"

"He's got a million and one," said Dawn.

Clay grinned. "Why was the painting arrested?"

"It was framed!" He and Olivia both said the punchline at the same time.

"Rabbit!" they shouted.

RABBIT!
RABBIT!

Amelia Bedelia giggled and got to work on another tote bag. She chose a T-shirt that said YOU GOTTA HAVE ART and started cutting.

"Hey," said Jackie, admiring her work. "I think that tote has my name on it!"

Amelia Bedelia took a look. "It doesn't yet," she said. "But I can fix that!"

"Thanks, Amelia Bedelia," said Jackie.

"You know . . ." she held up the dented ceiling light, "there's still time to transform this into something great before the show," she said.

Amelia Bedelia wrinkled her nose.

"What's wrong with it?" Olivia asked.

"That color is gross," said Amelia Bedelia.

A sly smile came over Olivia's face. "I know exactly how to fix that," she said.

Reaching into her backpack, she pulled out some cans of bright spray paint.

Dawn and Amelia Bedelia carried the ceiling light outside and spread out some newspaper. Amelia Bedelia chose a can of bright red paint.

"Before we paint it, we're going to sand it a bit, so the paint will stick better, and then wipe it clean," said Olivia. She handed Amelia Bedelia gloves and a mask. "The fumes from the spray paint are pretty powerful," she explained. "And you don't want to get paint on your hands. It's hard to get off." She held up her hands, which were splattered with pink paint.

Amelia Bedelia gasped. She had been right! Olivia had been caught pink-handed.

Olivia showed them how to spray smoothly and evenly and not to pause, which could result in drips.

"Great job!" said Olivia when they had finished.

"Is this what you used to do for your graffiti?' Amelia Bedelia asked.

Olivia nodded. "The paint comes out so quickly, and the cans are light and

easy to carry. Graffiti artists need to be fast!"

"I saw your new graffiti on the old factory," said Amelia Bedelia. "It's really pretty."

"Thanks," Olivia said. "That was my biggest one yet. I was having such a fun time creating it, I stopped paying attention to anything else . . . and that's how I got caught." She sighed. "I had to miss school and everything. My mom was really mad."

"School?" said Amelia Bedelia. "I thought you were a miner."

"I *am* a minor," Olivia replied. "That's why I'm still in school."

Amelia Bedelia hadn't realized there was a school in her town where you could learn mining. How interesting!

"What does S-A-S mean?" she asked.

Olivia looked embarrassed. "When I was little, my grandpa used to call me Sassy. I decided to make my tag SAS, kind of to honor him, you know?"

"That's really nice," said Amelia

Bedelia. "And thanks for teaching us how to spray paint. That was fun."

"Yeah," said Olivia. "But there's nothing like spraying a wall. That factory was the best. That huge space and all those empty walls. . . ." She sighed. "But they told me that if I am caught doing any more graffiti, I'll be in serious trouble. It won't matter that I am a minor."

Amelia Bedelia perked up. She was starting to get a very big idea.

Chapter 9

Painting the Floor Green

"Amelia Bedelia, you are a genius!" exclaimed Jackie.

"Actual geniuses are rare, but this idea is pretty smart!" said Amelia Bedelia.

They were standing in the courtyard of the old paint factory. Amelia Bedelia pulled her wagon to the center of the courtyard. The

wagon was loaded with different types of paint in different colors, as well as rakes, brushes, and brooms.

"It's just perfect," Jackie continued. "We can hang some of my sculptures from the lampposts and the gates. Let's arrange tables to display your upcycling projects, and maybe we can freshen everything up with some colorful paint."

"My uncle is a carpenter," said Daisy. "I bet he'd help us with tables."

"I wonder if we could barter with the gardening store," said Dawn. "Maybe we could trade some of our tin-can planters for some flowers."

"Wowzer!" said Jackie. "So many creative ideas!"

Amelia Bedelia and Jackie joined Olivia, who was studying the half-completed wall. She sighed. "I really wish I could have finished this one."

Amelia Bedelia turned to Jackie. "Why can't she?" she asked. "This place is probably getting torn down anyway."

"Well, I can always ask for permission," said Jackie. "Nothing ventured, nothing gained, right? If I get the go-ahead, then I don't see why not!"

"Are you serious?" said Olivia, her eyes wide.

Amelia Bedelia laughed. "She's never serious!" she said. "But she does want you to finish that wall!"

Olivia scampered up the ladder and began spraying the finishing touches on her work while Amelia Bedelia and her friends watched.

"It's way easier to paint when you don't have to look over your shoulder constantly!" she told them.

"But why do you do it if it's illegal and you can get in trouble?" asked Cliff.

"Where else can I get a canvas this big?" Olivia asked. "And an audience as wide as a whole town?"

Amelia Bedelia spun in a circle, looking around at the huge space. "Hey, why don't you paint all the walls?"

"Fabbityboo idea!" Jackie called from across the courtyard.

"But wouldn't a bunch of tags get pretty boring?" Olivia asked.

"Paint something else!" said Clay.

"Yeah," said Daisy. "You created those cool flowers. Why don't you paint more of those?"

Olivia considered this. "You know, that would look really awesome."

While Olivia got to work, Clay rummaged through the wagon and pulled out some half-empty cans of paint and some brushes. "Can we paint the benches?'" he asked Jackie.

"Paint whatever you like!" she replied. Amelia Bedelia pried the top off a can of paint. Inside was bright green. The far corner of the yard looked very dull. Maybe some grass would spruce it up!

After sweeping the cement, Amelia Bedelia knelt down and started painting. She lost herself in the back and forth, back and forth motion of the brush. It was hypnotizing.

"Earth to Amelia Bedelia!"

Amelia Bedelia looked up. Dawn was calling her.

"Amelia Bedelia, it looks like you have painted yourself into a corner!" she cried.

Yikes! Amelia Bedelia realized that she really *was* in a corner, with no place to go, surrounded by a lawn of wet green paint! She took a deep breath, then a flying leap. *Squish!* She left a trail of green footprints

almost all the way across the courtyard.

"I'm so sorry!" she said to Jackie. "What a mess."

"Are you kidding? I love it!" Jackie exclaimed. "Now everyone can follow in your footsteps!"

When Amelia Bedelia and her friends weren't decorating the courtyard, or watching Olivia paint, or bartering with area businesses, they were in the studio making more upcycling items. With over two hundred people expected, they had to be ready.

Amelia Bedelia ran out of T-shirts to make into totes, and materials to make pushpins and

magnets. She sighed and picked
up the ceiling light. It was now a
very cheerful (and shiny) shade
of red. But she still had no clue
how to transform it into art.

There must be *something* she could
use in this heap of treasure trash. Amelia
Bedelia started rooting around in the
piles. She peeked inside a paper
bag, closed it, then opened it up
again.

She had an idea. Something
that would honor the history of
the building. Was it too weird? No, it was
art! And Jackie always said you could
make art out of anything.

Amelia Bedelia got right to work.

When she was done, she stepped back
to admire her project.

"Hey, Olivia," she called. "Look at
this!"

"Wow," Olivia said. "I totally love it."

Amelia Bedelia smiled proudly. "I knew
you would," she said.

Chapter 10

An Amazetastic Art Show

Jackie checked her watch. "It's almost time," she said.

"I'm on pins and needles!" Alice cried.

"Then you should stand somewhere else!" said Amelia Bedelia.

"No, I mean I have butterflies in my stomach," said Alice.

Although Amelia Bedelia had

never eaten a butterfly, right now she could imagine what it might feel like.

"Amelia Bedelia," said Alice, hugging her friend, "can you believe how great this is?"

The upcycling art club was all set up for their show. Jackie's animal sculptures were displayed throughout the courtyard. They had borrowed sawhorses and plywood from Daisy's uncle and set up tables all around the courtyard to display their upcycled creations. Dawn, Cliff, and Clay had decorated the planters with

mosaics of broken china and filled them with donated flowers. Those, plus Olivia's flower graffiti, made the courtyard feel like a botanical garden. Olivia had painted trellises of roses, fields of wildflowers, a wall of ivy with pink blooms, and a lilac tree.

At noon the guests began to trickle in. Soon the courtyard was filled with friends, neighbors, teachers, and family.

Amelia Bedelia was in charge of the tote-bag table. She had carefully hand-lettered the sign: JUST SAY NO TO PLASTIC BAGS! GET YOUR T-SHIRT TOTES HERE!!

Amelia Bedelia's mother came up to her, holding a birdcage that had been transformed into a beautiful hanging basket. "Can you believe I just bought back my own birdcage?" she exclaimed, laughing. "This is going to look amazing in my office!"

"Dawn made that," said Amelia Bedelia proudly.

"Hey, Amelia Bedelia, these totes are a treat!" said Doris. She was a waitress down at Pete's Diner. She pulled a Pete's Diner T-shirt out of her bag. "This shirt has seen better days. Can you teach me how to make it into a tote bag?"

Amelia Bedelia began cutting. Then she had an idea. "Would you like the bottom to be flat or fringed?" she asked Doris.

UP-CYCLE ART

JUST SAY NO to PLASTIC BAGS GET YOUR T-SHIRT TOTES HERE!!

"Oh, fringed, please," said Doris. "That sounds fancy!"

Instead of turning the T-shirt inside out to tie the bottom, Amelia Bedelia tied it right-side out. In minutes, Doris had a new Earth-friendly tote bag with a fancy fringe!

Just then Amelia Bedelia spotted Mrs. Shauk in the crowd and remembered that she had made a special tote just for her. She reached underneath the table and pulled it out. It read HAWK'S AUTO REPAIR, with a big hawk, its wings outstretched, in the middle. She asked Cliff to keep an eye on her table while she crossed the courtyard to find her teacher.

Amelia Bedelia caught up to her

in front of Jackie's lion sculpture and tapped her on the shoulder. "I made this for you!" she said.

Mrs. Shauk turned around and gave Amelia Bedelia a quizzical look. "Shouldn't this be an eagle?" she asked, pointing to the bird with a pointy red fingernail. Amelia Bedelia blinked and looked closer. She had mistaken Regal the Eagle for her twin, Shauk the Hawk!

Mrs. Regal laughed. "I'll give this to my sister, Amelia Bedelia. Thanks!"

"Yoo-hoo! Helloppy!" Jackie called out to the crowd. Amelia Bedelia turned around. Jackie was standing in the center of the courtyard with the mayor. Today his bow tie was pink with purple polka dots. A purple pocket square and pink-and-purple striped socks completed his outfit.

"Thank you, Mr. Mayor, for coming to the first annual Upcycling Art Studio show!" Jackie said.

"We are here today because of you," the mayor told the crowd. "Your trash treasures have been saved from the landfill. And now we not only get to *reuse*

objects that would have been thrown away, but we are *reducing* the need to buy new things! It's good for our imaginations, our bank accounts, and our planet!"

"I would like to thank the upcycling club for all their hard work," said Jackie. "Special thanks to Amelia Bedelia for finding us this great space. And Olivia, you truly outdid yourself with your stunning murals."

The crowd burst into applause. Cliff whistled so loudly that Amelia Bedelia had

to cover her ears. Olivia blushed, turning bright pink.

"Now your face matches your hands," said Amelia Bedelia. "I'll introduce you to our mayor. He likes to match too!"

"We're so proud of Jackie and her amazing upcycling artists," said the mayor. "Please pat yourselves on the back! You've truly turned trash into treasure. And now I have a very important announcement to make, inspired by your club."

Amelia Bedelia patted herself on the back. She patted Dawn and Alice too, as the crowd grew quiet.

"The town council has voted to ban plastic bags in our town. Amelia Bedelia, you had better get cracking—we're going to need more tote bags!"

The day was a resounding success. Five of Jackie's

sculptures were sold, as well as every single upcycled item. Well, *almost* every single item. Amelia Bedelia's bright red ceiling light was the only thing left and looked very lonely indeed.

Amelia Bedelia picked it up, feeling disappointed.

"You just haven't found your audience yet," Jackie said from behind her. "Don't let this get you down in the dumps."

Amelia Bedelia brightened. "Let's head back there for more trash treasure as soon as we can!"

Chapter Eleven

The Writing Was on the Wall

Operation T-Shirt Tote Bag was in full swing. The whole class was making them. Amelia Bedelia had just finished her best one yet when there was a knock on the studio door.

"Amelia Bedelia, I think your mom's here!" said Clay. Amelia Bedelia looked up. It *was* her mom, and she looked very excited.

"What's going on?" Jackie asked as she opened the door.

"You have to come to the old paint factory to see for yourselves!"  Amelia Bedelia's mother said. "I can say no more. My lips are sealed."

"Oh no! With what?" asked Amelia Bedelia.

Amelia Bedelia's mother wouldn't say another word on the walk to the  factory, no matter how much Amelia Bedelia and her friends begged.

When they arrived, they walked through the archway into the courtyard. And there was the mayor, deep in

conversation with a man and a woman. The mayor waved them over.

"This is the upcycling art club I was telling you about," he said to the couple.

He turned to the group. "I wanted you guys to be the first to hear the news. Allow me to introduce you to Lisa and Ed Sweets. They are the owners of the art supply business that is coming to town. They've been looking for the right space for it. And then yesterday, they started seeing pictures of your art show in the news. And it gave them an idea. So now they want to—"

Amelia Bedelia couldn't help herself. "You want to move your company here!" she cried, interrupting the mayor.

"That's right," said Lisa. "What better spot for an art supply company than an old paint factory?"

"But what about the graffiti?" asked Olivia.

"We love it!" said Ed. "An art supply business needs plenty of beautiful artwork of all kinds."

"Even the tags?" Olivia asked.

"I can paint over those."

"We're called Sweets' Art Supply, so what do you think?" Lisa replied.

Everyone laughed. The SAS tags were perfect!

"I have a question," said Ed. "I spotted a photo of an amazing ceiling lamp decorated with paintbrushes," he said. "Is that still for sale, and can we get a dozen mobiles that feature lots of different art supplies?"

"I guarantee it!" said Amelia Bedelia, smiling at Jackie.

"There's one more thing," said the mayor.

"That's right," said Lisa. "The factory is a bit too big for us. So we'd like to rent out some of the extra space to another company." She paused dramatically. "We were thinking that maybe the Upcycling Art Studio—

and a shop to sell your products— would be a great fit."

"Oh, that's splenderiffic!" said Jackie. But then she frowned. "But . . . I don't know if I would be able to afford the rent."

"Well, here's the thing," said Ed. "We are an eco-friendly business, and we believe in your message. We'd be honored

$1.00 if you would be our tenant. So would rent of a dollar a month be acceptable?"

Jackie was speechless. She looked stunned.

Amelia Bedelia cleared her throat. "You might never take no for an answer, but you *can* take yes for an answer!"

Jackie blinked. "This is my dream come true," she said softly. "To be a full-time recycled-materials artist!"

Everyone cheered.

The mayor shook hands with Lisa and Ed, and then turned to Amelia Bedelia and her friends.

"Your creativity and vision have transformed this eyesore into a sight for sore eyes," he said.

Amelia Bedelia pointed to Olivia's giant tag. "When the newspaper first started reporting about Olivia's graffiti, the headline said, 'The Writing Is on the Wall,' like it was a bad thing. But actually it's the writing on the wall that has saved this paint factory and will help save our planet!"

Two Ways to Say It

By Amelia Bedelia

"I don't want to twist your arm."

"I don't want to make you do something you don't want to do."

"Close, but no cigar."

"Almost right."

"They will sell like hotcakes."

"They will sell quickly."

"You look like the cat that ate the canary."

"You look very pleased with yourself."

"It's the bee's knees!"

"It's amazing!"

"Shall we waive the reading?"

"Shall we agree not to read this out loud?"

"That has my name on it."

HAWK'S AUTO REPAIR

"That is perfect for me."

"You painted yourself into a corner."

"You got yourself into a difficult situation."

"My lips are sealed."

"I'm on pins and needles."

"I'm nervous."

145

"I won't say a word."

How to Make a ✦ T-Shirt Tote Bag ✦

Materials: T-shirt
Scissors (preferably fabric scissors)

Directions:

① Make the bag handles:

Lay the T-shirt on a flat surface and notice the seams that hold the sleeves onto the shirt. Cut off the sleeves, but leave the seams — that way the handles will be stronger.

② Make the bag opening:

Cut around the neck. Decide how wide you want your bag opening to be - if you want it to be a narrow opening, cut closer to the collar. Remember that it will stretch eventually.

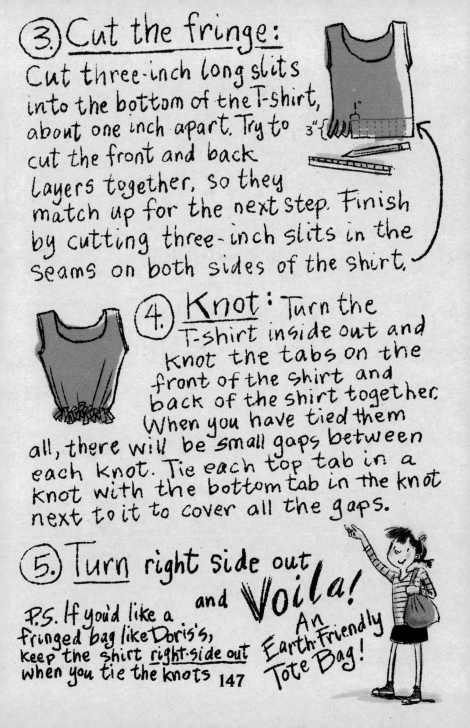

③ Cut the fringe:

Cut three-inch long slits into the bottom of the T-shirt, about one inch apart. Try to cut the front and back layers together, so they match up for the next step. Finish by cutting three-inch slits in the seams on both sides of the shirt.

④ Knot:

Turn the T-shirt inside out and knot the tabs on the front of the shirt and back of the shirt together. When you have tied them all, there will be small gaps between each knot. Tie each top tab in a knot with the bottom tab in the knot next to it to cover all the gaps.

⑤ Turn right side out and Voila!

An Earth-Friendly Tote Bag!

P.S. If you'd like a fringed bag like Doris's, keep the shirt right-side out when you tie the knots

147

Introducing...
Amelia Bedelia
& FRIENDS

Amelia Bedelia +
Good Friends =
Super Fun Stories
to Read and Share

1 Amelia Bedelia and her friends celebrate their school's birthday.

Amelia Bedelia and her friends discover a stray kitten on the playground!

2 *The Cat's Meow*

3 Amelia Bedelia and her friends take a school trip to the Middle Ages that is as different as knight and day.

4

Amelia Bedelia and her friends work to save Earth and beautify their town.

5

Coming soon . . .

149

The Amelia Bedelia Chapter Books

With Amelia Bedelia, anything can happen!

Have you read them all?